STAR WARS RESISTANCE

MEET THE PILOTS

WRITTEN BY ELLA PATRICK

ART BY LUCASFILM ANIMATION

DISNEY

LUCASFILM
PRESS

LOS ANGELES · NEW YORK

Printed in the United States of America

First Edition, January 2019   10 9 8 7 6 5 4 3 2 1

Library of Congress Control Number on file

FAC-029261-18334

ISBN 978-1-368-04452-3

Visit the official *Star Wars* website at: www.starwars.com.

SUSTAINABLE FORESTRY INITIATIVE

Certified Sourcing

www.sfiprogram.org
SFI-01415

Meet Kaz.

Kaz is a pilot for the New Republic.

But Kaz is looking for a new adventure.

Kaz meets Resistance pilot
Poe Dameron.

Together they take on a strange
red First Order TIE fighter.
But the red TIE gets away.

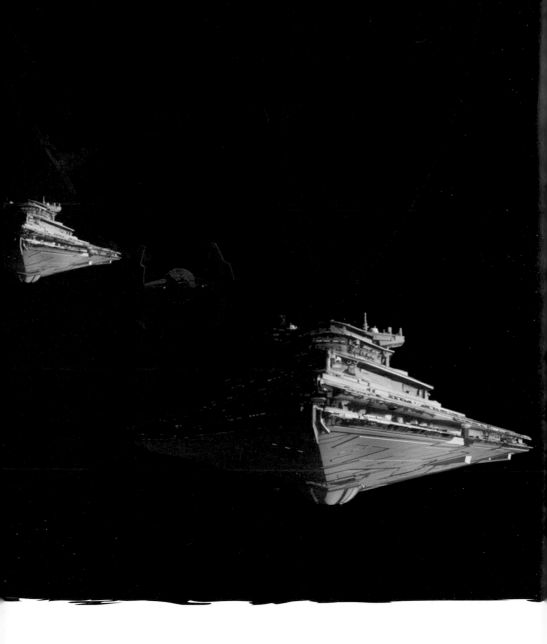

The First Order is a growing threat in the galaxy.

Leia Organa's Resistance needs
information about the First Order.
Leia and Poe ask Kaz to be
a spy for the Resistance.

Welcome to the Colossus!
The Colossus is a fueling station
that floats on a water planet.

Pilots, pirates, spies, droids,
and aliens of all kinds stop here
to rest and refuel.

Kaz will live on the Colossus
to spy on the First Order.

But Kaz is not alone.

Poe's friendly droid, BB-8,

stays with him.

Kaz and BB-8 report to Yeager.

Yeager runs a repair shop

on the Colossus.

He is an old friend of Poe's.

Kaz will work for Yeager
to blend in on the Colossus.
No one can know that
Kaz is a spy.

Neeku, Tam, and Bucket also
work with Yeager.
Neeku is a kind alien.

Tam is a mechanic who
hopes to be a pilot one day.
And Bucket is a silly old droid.

Meet the Aces.

These top pilots race around
the Colossus for sport.

Hype Fazon is an alien who loves to be the center of attention.

Griff Halloran's ship is part Imperial TIE.

Freya Fenris flies a fiery-red ship.

Bo Keevil is a quiet racer,
but he's lightning fast.

Torra Doza is the youngest Ace
and the most daring pilot.
Torra's father, Captain Doza,
runs the Colossus.

Kaz loves watching the
Aces race.

He hopes one day he can be
an Ace, too.

Meet Flix and Orka.

Flix is tall.

Orka is short.

Flix and Orka help racers and mechanics get the parts they need for their ships.

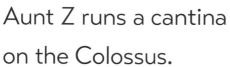

Aunt Z runs a cantina
on the Colossus.

Bolza Grool
makes sure
everyone pays
Aunt Z.

The Aces also protect
the Colossus from pirates.

An alien named Kragan leads
the gang of pirates.

They steal parts to create
their deadly ships.

The pirates try to attack
the Colossus to steal fuel.

But the Aces scare them off!

Major Vonreg and Commander Pyre
arrive on the Colossus.
Vonreg is the pilot of the red TIE.
Pyre is a trooper in golden armor.

Vonreg and Pyre report to
Captain Phasma.

The First Order is

certainly up to something. . . .

Kaz will have to work hard to
stay on top of the First Order.
And he will have to work even harder
to train to become an Ace.

One thing is for sure:
Kaz and the pilots are
in for an adventure!